WHERE'S BLUEY?

A SEARCH-AND-FIND BOOK

THE BEACH

The beach is the perfect place to spend a hot summer's day. But don't forget your sunscreen!

Can you find:

Bingo

Bluey

a pair of red thongs (that's Australian for flip-flops!)

a pink spade

a pelican

Bluey's shell

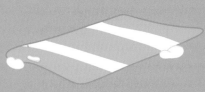
a green stripy towel

a bottle of sunscreen

SLEEPYTIME

Bingo is asleep and dreaming of space. *Shh . . .* Try not to wake her up!

Can you find:

Saturn

three glow-in-the-dark stars

Floppy

an asteroid shaped like . . .

a pine cone

a penguin

a gnome

an octopus

THE PLAYGROUND

The playground is so much fun. Bluey and Bingo could spend the whole day here.

Can you find:

Bluey's bike

Bluey's helmet

Muffin's drink bottle

a galah

a cockatoo

an adventure swag

a picnic basket

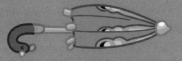
an umbrella

BBQ IN THE PARK

Bluey and her friends are playing a spy game while their parents picnic by the river. Time to go on a mission!

Can you find:

Chloe

Mackenzie

Honey

a tennis ball

a cooler

three pine cones

a pile of stones

a tomato sauce bottle

an Aussie football

CAMPING

The Heeler family are on a camping holiday! It's almost time for dinner, but Bluey and Jean Luc are nowhere to be seen.

Can you find:

Bluey

Jean Luc

Muffin's backpack

a stick tent

three orange flower bushes

a yellow bucket

a bunny night light

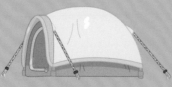

the Heelers' tent

PLAYROOM

What a mess! Muffin and Socks have come to visit and are lost among all of Bluey and Bingo's toys.

Can you find:

Muffin

Socks

a cloud bag

Bob Bilby

a red balloon

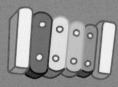

a xylophone

an octopus toy

a tartan hat

BLUEY AND BINGO'S BEDROOM

Muffin is having a sleepover with Bluey and Bingo. It's so exciting, no one wants to go to bed!

Can you find:

Bluey

Bingo

Muffin

two sleepy cloud pillows

a sleeping bag

Bluey's pillow

a storybook

a fruit bat

a photo of Bluey and Bingo

THE NEIGHBOURHOOD

What a busy neighbourhood. Bluey loves playing with her friends!

Can you find:

Judo

Lucky

three recycling bins

Lucky's dad

a tree with orange flowers

Bluey's bike

Bluey and Bingo's red wagon

a garden gnome

a turtle-shaped cloud

THE BACKYARD

Bluey and Bingo have lots of fun in their backyard. It can be anything they want it to be . . . a zoo, an island or the perfect place to play mah-jong!

Can you find:

five garden gnomes

a giraffe drawing

three socks

a stripy ball

a ladybird

a skipping rope

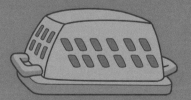

a laundry basket

AT SCHOOL

It's playtime at school. Check out the Terriers' fort and Honey's gnome village. *Whoa!*

Can you find:

the three Terriers

two hobby horses

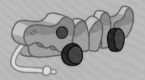

a crocodile toy

three gnomes

Calypso's braided bracelet

a pile of wooden craft sticks

two yellow cushions

BBQ

The Heelers are having a BBQ on the back deck . . . but after Bingo makes her salad, nothing is quite where it should be!

Can you find:

five yellow flowers

a BBQ sauce bottle

a tray of sausages

Bandit's water bottle

Bingo's relaxer chair

three plates

two seed pods

HEELERS' FRONT DOOR

Bluey and Bingo can't possibly leave the house until they've found some of their things!

Can you find:

five sticky geckos

Mum's keys

a double-decker bus

Bingo's toothbrush

Bluey's hat

an Australia pin

Mum's phone

AT THE MARKET

Visiting the market is so much fun, especially when you have some dollarbucks to spend!

Can you find:

four ponies

a mustard sauce bottle

a blue kite

three wind chimes

a toffee apple

a guitar

BLUEY AND HER FRIENDS

Congratulations!
You've found everything!

Can you find:

BLUEY

(Watch out for the fake Blueys!)

Did you spot
Long Dog on
every page, too?

ANSWERS